MITZVAH PIZZA

FOR SWEET ALEX,
FOREVER IN OUR HEARTS - S.L.S.

TO LARRY AND MACK,
WHO MAKE ME LAUGH EVERY DAY - D.M.

Backmatter photograph is courtesy of Mason Wartman

KAR-BEN PUBLISHING, INC.
A division of Lerner Publishing Group, Inc.
241 First Avenue North
Minneapolis, MN 55401 USA
1-800-4-KARBEN

Website address: www.karben.com

Main body text set in Avenir LT Pro 16/20.
Typeface provided by Linotype AG.

Library of Congress Cataloging-in-Publication Data

Names: Scheerger, Sarah Lynn, 1975- author. | Melmon, Deborah, illustrator.
Title: Mitzvah pizza / by Sarah Lynn Scheerger ; illustrated by Deborah Melmon.
Description: Minneapolis : Kar-Ben Publishing, [2019] | Series: Jewish values | Summary: Missy is trying to decide what to buy during her weekly Daddy Day when she meets a new friend and learns she can buy pizza for people who cannot afford a slice. Includes facts about Rosa's Fresh Pizza in Philadelphia.
Identifiers: LCCN 2018007311 (print) | LCCN 2018014500 (ebook) | ISBN 9781541542150 (eb pdf) | ISBN 9781541521704 (lb : alk. paper) | ISBN 9781541521711 (pb : alk. paper)
Subjects: | CYAC: Generosity—Fiction. | Commandments (Judaism)—Fiction. | Friendship—Fiction. | Fathers and daughters—Fiction. | Jews—United States—Fiction. | Pizza—Fiction.
Classification: LCC PZ7.S34244 (ebook) | LCC PZ7.S34244 Mit 2019 (print) | DDC [E]—dc23

LC record available at https://lccn.loc.gov/2018007311

PJ Library Edition ISBN 978-1-5415-6296-7

Manufactured in China
2-1008988-47537-10/18/2022

0623/B1347/A6

MITZVAH PIZZA

Pizza 4u ♥ Missy

Pizza is the best!

FREE PIZZA

SARAH LYNN SCHEERGER

ILLUSTRATED BY DEBORAH MELMON

KAR-BEN PUBLISHING

"Ready to go, Missy?"
Daddy asks.

"Yes!" I squeal. It's Daddy Day.
The best day of the week!

Daddy brings the money.
I bring the fun.

Usually.

Today, *I'm* bringing the money *and* the fun. I've been saving up since Hanukkah. I even did extra chores.

On the crowded Philly sidewalks, I swing hands with Daddy. He asks me how I want to spend my money.

I haven't decided yet.

One time I decided to buy a beaded necklace.

It broke.

Another time I decided to buy cinnamon candies.

They burned my tongue.

And another time I decided to buy my friend's half-used clay. I forgot to check whether it had gotten crusty, clumpy, or dry.

Oops.

Deciding is hard work. So we're taking a break to eat. Pizza!

As we get in line, the smell of melted cheese, bubbling sauce, and warm dough makes my mouth water. *Mmm.*

The girl in front of us is with her daddy, too.
"What would you like?" our dads ask at the same time.
"Mushroom!" she cheers, doing the pizza dance.
"Cheese!" I say, and I twirl for emphasis.
We look at each other.

"Cheese is better," I say.
"Mushroom," she counters.

I’m right, of course.
“My name is Melissa,” I tell her, “but everyone calls me Missy.”
“And I’m Jane. But everyone calls me Jane.”
We smile at each other, big and wide.

We're almost to the front of the line. "Grab us two," Jane's dad says. Jane trots over to a wall plastered with sticky notes—the kind Mom uses to leave us reminders on the fridge.

"Two mushroom slices, please," Jane says, handing two sticky notes to the man behind the counter.

I nudge Daddy. "I don't understand. Pizza for sticky notes?"

Jane whirls to face me. "Each sticky note is a piece of pizza."

That's the strangest thing I've ever heard.

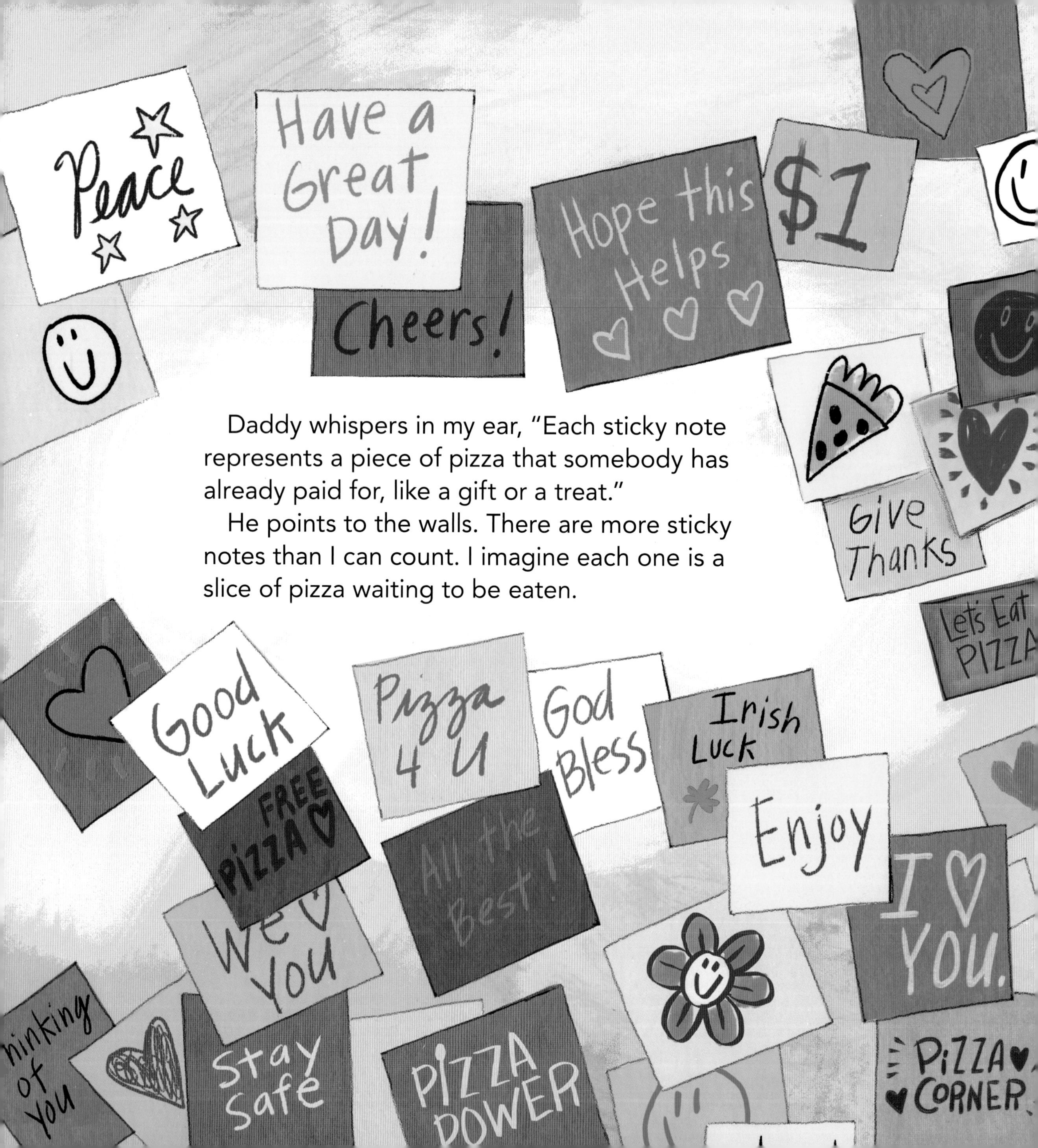

Daddy whispers in my ear, "Each sticky note represents a piece of pizza that somebody has already paid for, like a gift or a treat."

He points to the walls. There are more sticky notes than I can count. I imagine each one is a slice of pizza waiting to be eaten.

So many, they almost make me dizzy.

Jane finds a seat, flashing me her slice of mushroom with a thumbs up. I shake my head and point to the cheese slice on the menu. Cheese is way better.

Daddy orders our slices, and I pay two dollars. "It's my treat," I tell him.

The man behind the counter asks Daddy, "Would you like to make a donation to the Piece O'Pizza Fund?"

"Sure," Daddy says. He pulls out a dollar. "It's a mitzvah," he says with a wink.

Mitzvah means "good deed" in Hebrew.

He starts to write on the sticky note, but I tug his sleeve.

"Can I write the message, Daddy?"

He smiles.

I use the markers from a jar on the counter to make a rainbow at the top of the paper. Underneath it, I draw a slice of cheese pizza. The best kind.

I peek at Jane. She looks away real fast and smiles at her mushroom.

I stick the note to the wall.

Daddy and I sit by the window, chewing.

"Thank you for lunch. Did you decide what to do with the rest of your money?" asks Daddy.

I shake my head "no" because my mouth is full, and so is my head. There are too many choices.

"We're going to the park," Jane calls to me from her table.

I don't want to say good-bye to my new friend yet. "Can we go too, Daddy?"

"Of course," he says. "You're in charge of the fun, remember?"

At the park, Jane and I swing until our feet touch the sky. We slide, climb and jump.

We spin and we twirl.

We holler and we laugh until our sides ache.

I tell her about the party we're planning for my birthday next week. "Wanna come?" I ask my new friend. "We'll have pizza, lemonade, and cupcakes!"

She asks her dad if she can come, and I'm so happy when he says, "Yes."

"I'll save a slice for you," I promise her. "Mushroom, of course."

Jane's favorite color is red, and mine is purple. She likes mushroom, and I like cheese. She pays with sticky notes, and I pay with dollars. We're not so different.

Suddenly I know how I want to spend the rest of my money.

After I wave good-bye to Jane and her dad, I run over to the bench where Daddy is sitting.

"Let's go back to The Pizza Corner. I have a mitzvah in mind." I'm smiling so wide that I think I'll crack my face. Daddy and I swing hands all the way back to The Pizza Corner. I stop a few times to twirl.

At The Pizza Corner, I trade five dollars for five sticky notes. I write something different on each one, using every marker in the jar. I stick them to the wall, clustering them together like friends.

"Thanks for the pizza and the fun, Missy."
Daddy hugs me. "Next time, I'll treat."
I kiss his scratchy cheek.

HAPPY BIRTHDAY MISSY

Author's Note

Rosa's Fresh Pizza, on which The Pizza Corner in this story is based, is a real place. It is located in Philadelphia. The owner, Mason Wartman, traded the busy world on Wall Street for the cheese-filled world of pizza making. When he left stock trading to run his own business, he decided to open a pizza shop. He'd seen the success of one dollar pizza shops when he had lived in Manhattan, and he wanted to bring that idea to Philadelphia.

One day a customer asked if he could buy a slice of pizza for someone who couldn't afford one. This sparked an idea. Mason Wartman brought sticky notes to his shop and used them to symbolize free slices of pizza. Each sticky note represented one pre-purchased slice of pizza.

Now he serves free pizza to thirty to forty hungry people every day. Eventually he hired some of them to work in the shop, further helping them to live independently.

The walls of the pizza shop are covered with a rainbow of sticky notes, each with a different, positive message from people wanting to make a difference in the world.

Mason Wartman